I0712457

BERJA
J.K. DIVIA

Paperback ISBN: 979-8-9875277-3-3
eBook ISBN: 979-8-9875277-4-0

Cover Art and Illustrations: Zooe Franci

Final Editing and formatting by Odyssey Inkworks

Cover: Shawn Morrow, Ph.D.

Dedication

To my family, especially my husband and mother, for all their support and help in continuing to make this Author dream of mine a reality. To the friends who encouraged me throughout this journey and kept pushing me to keep going. To everyone who was part of the Berja writing process, from beta readers to the early editors, my ARC readers and fellow author friends.

To my kids for being the best, seriously they're awesome.

Finally, to my big brother, for letting me honor him on his birthday by releasing my Dark Fantasy novella full of human sacrifice and woe on his special day, love you!

Thank you for everything.

Chapters

Berja

By

J.K Divia

The Way of the Forest Gods

Once, we lived in darkness, deep in caves not far from here. There was only one season, and it was one of death. That was before we followed the Forest Gods; before they showed us the way and the stone altar built. To receive the forest's blessing, we must go through the seasons with it. We must offer up our own, the first children of spring or a child born of the Forest Gods, for blessings or blood.

Chapter

1

The Nest

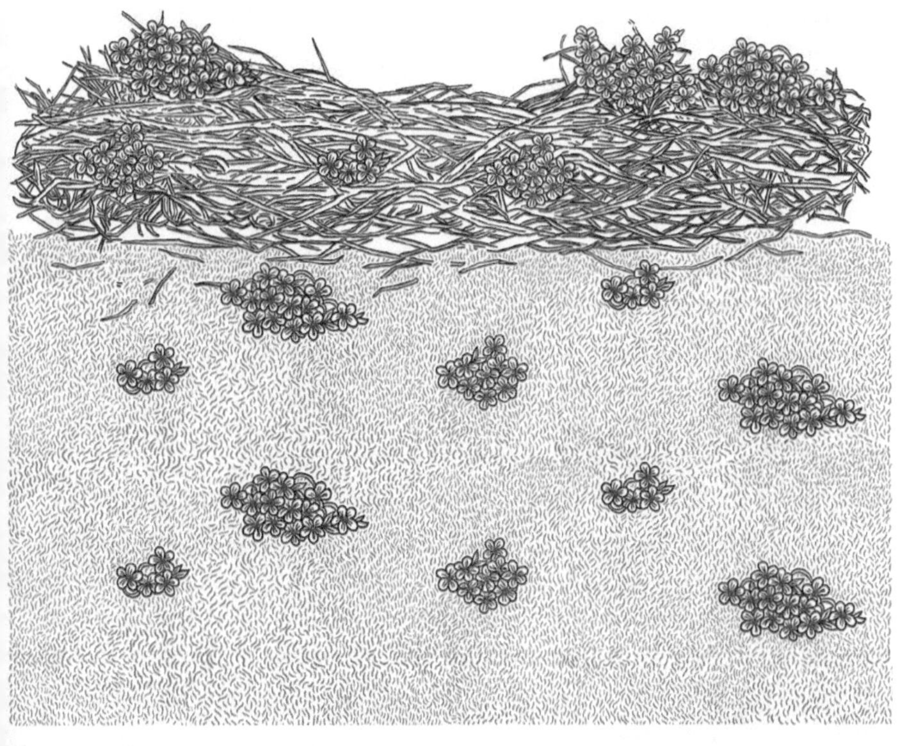

Tonight, I will run.

This giant nest of dried out branches and straw won't keep me.

I know what is ahead of me if I stay. I have watched it every year since I was a child.

I have paid attention.

They say it is an honor, but what they mean is that it is a duty for me as a daughter. A sale by my family. They were pleased when I was chosen as the Spring Maid. They knew it meant their bellies would remain full this year, regardless of whether I lived or died.

The space around me is filled with the movement of preparation for tomorrow. Fragrant herbs and laced fresh flowers in whites, yellows and pinks adorn the nest. Hands flock to pick and pull my dark hair apart like little birds, weaving it together as I sit prettily in the nest, feigning obedience.

"Drekka," they urge me, pushing a small wooden bowl with intricate carvings to my mouth.

The carvings show the cycle of the seasons: of life, death, and rebirth. I am meant to mark the end of death, to usher in the rebirth of the village.

My lips feel fuzzy as the sickly-sweet smelling liquid unsuccessfully searches for a way inside.

The drink is meant to ease my nerves and dull my senses. To ease the pain and fear. To make us, the chosen Spring Maids, submit willingly to what awaits us in the forest. To what we must endure before we enter the dark, tall tree line.

Braided locks of my hair fall one by one against my back with gentle thuds as each set of hands flies away to attend to another task. The village men, the strongest warriors, file in one by one and take their place around the nest, like predators circling their prey. Their breath in the cold morning air creates a fog that threatens to smother me like smoke from a fire. They believe me to be a helpless bird, like the little blackbird that sits upon the mistletoe, staring at me with bright green eyes. None of them believe that I would dare fly away. They brush my actions off as nerves, harmless as the trembles from a newborn calf seeking and failing to find its first footing.

When I do escape, maybe the little bird will help lead my way.

I smile at him, and those green eyes smile back. They say he is a bad omen, that he foretells of death, and maybe he does because he appeared the day I was chosen. He is my only friend though, besides the little straw doll we have made together over the last few weeks. The little bird is the only one who brings me gifts——tiny piles of berries and smooth rocks that sit hidden in the nest beside me. He doesn't sing like other birds though, but rather looks down upon us and laughs when they try to chase him away. If it is my death that he is warning of, at least it comes upon a friendly face, a laugh, and his company.

My body rests easily upon my bare feet and legs that lie under my long, green linen dress as I sit upright in the nest. I stretch my head and neck above the nest walls and look toward the sky. As we near closer to the start of spring, the sun begins to linger just a bit longer above me.

The Elder comes and I tuck my little doll under the lip of the nest. I will not share her with anyone. The Elder lightly lays her gnarled hands upon my shoulders to push me back into my captivity. There are no others as old as her in the village. None with as many lines in their face or rings on their body. Soon, she will take her place in the forest at the base of the oldest tree, whose trunk is as wide as four men and its height we cannot tell. When she lays amongst its roots and becomes a part of it, another will assume the role of Elder, and the cycle will continue as it has for countless seasons.

The South Men follow no such cycle. They only take. They only kill. They never give back. Their seasons are only that of harvest and death. They have no Spring Children and no Forest Gods. I wonder what that freedom is like, to not be beholden to someone or something.

They say that is why the South Men are cursed to always move and encroach upon others; setting up only to leave for the next place to take from. Why their roots are weak and constantly seeking the water and fertile soils of others and moving on once they have depleted the land. Why they have been coming up further north, though they fear what lives in our dark woods: our Forest Spirits and Gods.

The Elders say there is nothing to fear when you give the Forest what it desires; when you awaken it with gifts of Spring Maids, and when that doesn't work, then with the blood of Spring Children upon the fields and altar.

The burning sensation builds in my thighs and stomach as she pushes harder. My body holds, resisting her, and I smile.

"Drekka?" she asks another elder woman.

Shaking her head of long grey hair, she places the still-filled bowl into the Elder's outstretched hand. With the cluck of her tongue, pain begins to grow in my cheeks as the branch-like fingers of the Elder's hand shoot around my chin and take root in my skin. She tries to force my lips apart, but I only smile. I take the pain as the flood of liquid brings again the feeling of fuzziness to my lips as I deny entry once more. Another cluck, and her sharp fingertips pull away from my skin, leaving behind only their sting. My still hands rest upon my lap, and I keep my gaze fixed forward. My little bird friend laughs again from the mistletoe branch, and I resist the urge to laugh with him at my defiance, or my folly.

Drink or not, the ritual continues, and I feel the air move in with the men who come into the nest with me. Their fingers attempt to take root in my skin from the many branches of outstretched arms that surround me and try to pull me down into submission.

I am rigid.

I am unyielding.

The seeds cannot be planted if the Spring Maid is unwilling. Their attempts will bear no fruit. No seeds will be planted—seeds that will grow to become new Spring Maids, sacrifices, or servants to the village. Seeds that will never be allowed to be free, but only grow to serve one single purpose, one that offers no joy.

No control.

No sense of self.

No name beyond that of Spring Child and then Spring Maid if chosen by the Elder.

We who are born of Spring Maids are like saplings forced with bindings to grow in specific patterns to please and support the village. To appease the Forest Gods and mark the beginning of the hunting season in the woods. To symbolize the earths rebirth after it's long winters death. I'd much prefer the quick press of a blade against my skin or heart than surrender to my duty. To surrender to a life of sacrifice.

The drink has always ensured our acceptance, softening our fields for planting.

I have taken no drink.

I do not accept my fate, and they cannot force me.

Chapter
2

Once a
Spring Maid

A light in the darkness reaches out through the thicket of branch-like limbs from the village warriors who grab at me. With their reach comes another cluck of the Elder's tongue. The trees pull back their branches and roots, and my nest is once again my own.

I break my upward gaze to look for my green-eyed companion, my Little Bird, but am left only with her who was once a Spring Maid herself. The light in the darkness is no beacon of hope, no guiding light to safety, but rather one that leads to treacherous waters like the turbulent flow of the spring rivers that feed the Fjord, waiting to drown me.

It is my mother.

Waiting for her to speak to me, my stomach drops. It falls deep into my body the way it always does when I both hope for and fear her attention. When I long for her touch but never dare to ask or initiate contact the way her children, born of the village, are able to do without care or thought. The ones who I long to love and be loved by but am forced to be separated from in both affection and bond though we share the same mother. I sit in the corner, alone, and watch them bloom in her light. I sometimes wonder what it would be like to be loved by them, to be loved by her. To be allowed to grow beyond the confines of my duty. What I would do if given that chance.

"If it were not for your beauty, they would think you were part troll from your behavior. Or worse yet, a South Man. Need we worry about you placing a blade upon our throats as we sleep?" She comes to stand before me and grabs a lock of my hair. My scalp prickles at the touch I can almost feel.

"I try to think of what I could have done to make you hate me so," she says. The lock of my dark hair falls from her scarred hand—the only sign from her time in the forest besides me—as she comes to sit before the nest. Only her head is visible to me now from inside the nest walls.

"I wonder what it would be like to be allowed to feel," I snap back. I keep perfectly still in my nest, eyes forward, hands clasped as I was taught to do. As I am only allowed to do.

"Your defiance does not make you brave. It does not make you better than the rest of us, better than me. I have been where you are, Spring Maid. I know exactly what it is like to sit there in that nest. To be poked and prodded."

She places her hands on top of the nest wall, lifting herself up so we are face to face.

"I did it," she says.

I refuse to acknowledge the sting of her fingers that suddenly dig into my chin as she pulls my face closer to hers and I am forced to look at her, at what I can become if I give up, give in. If I accept my fate and am blessed.

"I did what was asked, what was required, what we were both born for. What you are doing is not survival, not for you or the village. I thought you were capable of love, even if you had none for me." The pain of her touch still lingers, though her fingers have receded like flood waters.

"I thought maybe you had love for that Spring Child who works the fields with the other men though. The one with the copper hair that shines brilliantly in the sun. The way you two look at each other, the way you stare when you think no one is looking, I can see the wanting. But this proves you do not. You are selfish," Mother states.

My body tenses and I adjust my position. How could she know about him, who I call Eemil? I have often dreamed of a life together, one where we have names and freedom. I have spoken to no one of him. I speak to no one in general—the law forbids it beyond my own family.

"I am not allowed to love, though I have only ever wanted to. Wished to," I reply. The skin of my clasped hands becomes white from my tightened grip.

"If you only knew the true blessing of not loving, of not feeling. With love also comes anger, fear, and grief. Do you think you are strong enough to bear those feelings? To handle that kind of pain? I think not. Consider yourself a blessed child and surrender to the moment you were created for. Do it well and with honor and maybe, just maybe, the Gods will smile upon you as they did me and we will see you back. Then you will be able to feel what you say you have desired for so long. Then you will see that maybe it was better to not have known after all and you will come to thank me for sparing you that burden." She places one hand on top of the nest wall in front of me. I resist the sudden urge to reach out and touch her.

"I've never heard you refer to me as a blessing before."

"I did not. It remains to be seen if you are so," she says and reaches her arm into the nest to pick up a lock of my hair in her slender fingers once again. Mother starts to roll it between her thumb and forefinger.

"You have never loved me. Not even when you came back and were free to do so. Why should I surrender for something which has never shown me love?" I knock back her hand, shocking us both as I free myself from her touch—something that I once craved for more than anything.

"What sense is there in loving something that will never be yours? You were destined to be a Spring Maid the moment I laid upon the cold stone altar, seeded and sown. I knew when you were born you would end up in this nest. I couldn't change that any more than my mother could change it for me.

"You were never mine. You were a duty that I fulfilled. I did what was asked. I submitted to my task. I survived it on my own. For a new moon cycle, I was out there in the woods, praying to the gods. I waited for the moon to be full and beckon me home if I did not bleed. When it came and there was no blood, I was able to come back. I carried you. I bore you as was my duty, and I was able to take my place in the village as a free woman, as a named one, no longer a Spring Maid."

She stands before me, looking down as she has done my whole life, and adds, "You know nothing of surviving, Spring Maid."

"It was your job to teach me," I say.

"No one taught me. It is up to the Forest Gods if you live or not. Not up to me, not up to you. The moment you were born I knew you were not mine, you belonged to the village, to the Forest Gods. Your worth is tied into being the Spring Maid and fulfilling those duties, as were mine. Do them, let the seeds be sown, and come back as I did. If you are strong enough. If you are worthy enough. Or accept your fate with grace, with bravery, with love for your family and village who have kept you well for this moment. Do it to honor the Forest Gods who led our people out of darkness and death," Mother states boldly.

"Worthy to sacrifice but not to love," I remark.

"Succeed in your duty and you will be. If that is not enough, if you can think of no other reason, then think of the poor Spring Child who you hold affection for. Does he deserve to die? If the crops fail and the snares and nets are empty, if the South Men continue to take from the forest and our people, then another sacrifice will be given—one in blood."

"Our love can never be," I say.

"Yes, and what is the point in loving something that will never be yours? Now, you see." There is no pity in her voice, no sympathy as she asks, "What will you do, Spring Maid?"

Silence is my answer.

"Our destiny is set whether we cooperate or not. You are the Spring Maid. If not for the sake of us, then for your own sake, take the drink the Elder offers, do your part in the ritual. Bring honor to yourself since you will not do it for us, or face the darkness alone," she tells me before turning away.

"I will face it alone, regardless," I whisper.

She calls one last time over her shoulder, not looking at me, "It is not me that you shame, only yourself."

They say it is an honor, but how can there be honor without a choice? Why was I born without a choice? They say the past is no more fixed than our future in some ways, that each day there is an ability to create a new past. But that is not so for those born of the Spring Maids; we are penned animals awaiting slaughter. I dream of being more, of being free. Of being loved and a part of something, not put aside or apart from the rest. Of being better than those I had come from.

Without another word, my mother leaves, and with every step she takes away from me, my body relaxes a little more and the breath I've been holding returns.

Chapter
3

A Mother
in Dreams

Berja

The varying shades of brown and grey twigs and branches of the nest poke and prod like the fingers of the villagers who have given up on their attempts to drug and seed me. I let out a deep sigh and take my little doll out of hiding. I bring her to my chest, wishing she was made of skin and bone and not twigs and straw. I wish that I had made her out of love with Eemil instead of my loneliness and scavenged gifts from Little Bird. Pressing my lips against the top of her little wood head, I lay down as my heavy body begins to prickle and buzz and the heaviness of sleep becomes too much to fight. This will be the last time I sleep in the safety of the nest that cages me.

My green-eyed friend, my Little Bird, caws gently before flying away. Just a quick rest before tonight, when my little doll and I will run south. Should the South Men find me, it will be a death from that of my own choices, unlike the one that awaits me on the cold stone altar. That is where it ends for most Spring Maids, the ones who fail to bear the fruit from the seeds planted during the ceremony.

The nights are getting shorter, and I must make use of the time I have with them. My heavy eyes close and a woman begins to take shape. I hear her call to me, telling me to run.

"Berja," she calls with bright red lips like fresh blood from an offering to the Forest Gods.

"Will you submit?" she asks.

My heart races at her voice, at the name she calls me. Her dark hair is a flowing river that I wish I could disappear in. Everything about her is beautiful and terrifying but it's more than that. With the darkness and in her depths is an echo of freedom. It is inviting, and I drink from the waters of her words that flow from those red lips with a thirst that can't be quenched. I will not submit. I want my freedom. I want the name she calls me.

I want to live for me.

My feet feel light as I stand up, dropping my doll and stepping over the tall nest wall to the ground that is a mix of cold hardness and wet softness as the earth awakens. I walk toward the edge of the dark forest, sometimes sinking in the thawing earth, sometimes shivering from the frigid air of the moonless path to her, to the altar I know she is at. Her voice calls me closer. Closer to what feels like freedom, like my destiny.

"Berja," she calls, "will you submit?"

I break into a run, shouting, "No!"

I will not. I will not submit to my fate.

I run, but time does not seem to exist here. The forest path ends, splitting into two clearings. Ahead, I can see a hard, rocky path that ends at the foot of a dark cave entrance.

Glowing fragments of tiny, bleached bones peek out from within the cave. I wonder if this is the place the Forest Gods led us from all those seasons ago. Is this cave the dry mouth of death the Spring Maids sprang into life from? I need to see. I need to know why we fled from here.

Turning toward the illuminated bones, pain creeps up from the bottom of my bare feet from each step I take onto the hard, frozen earth. There is a dark shadow lurking just inside the cave, past where I can see. I can sense its insatiable hunger, and it fills me with fear.

"Berja," she calls again.

Her voice pulls me back safely to her with a haunting melody I cannot rid myself of. My fear subsides as her voice breathes life into my heart and soul, and warmth begins to grow inside me. The pain subsides as the freezing cold path gives way to the softer ground of the forest. When I finally reach her, the pain is just a memory.

Her smile stokes the fire from the spark she created inside me as she glides around the large stone slab of the altar, dark blue dress swinging as she does, asking, "What will you do?"

"I will run," I state firmly.

"Running is not enough," she replies.

"I will run, and I will live for me!" I shout loud enough for all the gods and the spirits in the forest to hear. They need to know that I reject them.

"Run south and the South Men will catch you. You will be forced to serve and worse. But run down the forest path, Berja, and you will find a man, a bear, and a god. He will offer you a choice. He will offer you a voice, powerful words. You must be careful with them, and who you share them with. They will take your words but not their meaning." She comes to stand before me, stretching out her arm, stretching out her fingers to gently and lovingly caress my face in the way I had always dreamed of my own mother doing, but there is a heaviness in her gaze.

"They will make you a mother of monsters and lead your children to a place you cannot follow," she says.

Chapter
4

Forest God

I will be a mother.

That is the last thing running through my mind before the echoes of her voice abruptly end and the sharp caw of a bird brings me out of the dream with a start. I sit up in the nest, my heart beating painfully, ears filled with the sound of the Elder's song, and I know my time is up. The final part of the ceremony has begun, and I will have to leave the nest, my prison, and face something worse.

I put my hand down to steady myself, then quickly pull it back at the feeling of something cold and wet beneath my fingers. I move my hand and see my little doll is covered in blood. No, I look closer, it is berries. The Little Bird laughs and I know what I must do to escape. I grab the berries and tuck my ruined doll down into the nest. Quietly, I smash the berries in my hands, getting as much juice as I can on my legs and dress, turning them bright red like fresh blood.

I stand up and the singing turns to wailing. Multiple hands flock to the nest and to me. It is an omen, they cry, one that means my blood must be spilled upon the fields now that I will not bear fruit, and upon the altar. My mother is there amongst the other village women, all dressed in white, all reaching and wailing with outstretched arms. Flowers that they once held are now strewn across the ground.

All except one, a dark-haired girl who is younger than me, a Spring Child. She stands in defiance amongst the fallen village women, and a crowd of older Spring Children begin to gather behind her. Smiling, she mouths the word, '*Run.*'

The Elder stands before the nest, blocking my path. She already carries the large knife used to free the blood of sacrifices in her hand, and the village men stand behind her, waiting. My heart beats aggressively in my chest, desperate to flee without me. I stand frozen, until the Elder screams. The little blackbird, my friend, attacks her face with the beating of his wings. It is now that I must run. There is no choice for me on what path to take. There is only one before me, and I must go or they will catch me and cut me open, sprinkling my blood upon the fields and laying my bones upon the altar.

To the forest path I run. I look back and see the village gathered behind me, the dark-haired girl continuing to smile, and my Eemil standing still in the back. No one has given chase yet. My green-eyed friend, my Little Bird, flies above me, laughing all the way.

The brown and yellow spring earth is damp beneath my feet. I slide in the thick, cold, dark mud, but I refuse to fall as my body lurches forward every few steps. The path is narrow, and I know where it will lead. I run faster, my throat and chest burning from the chilly air. A sharp pain in my side almost makes me double over, and my legs cramp and protest their sudden use after my time in the nest, but I push past it and keep running.

The woods are quiet this morning, save for the sound of my feet and heavy breaths. The little blackbird did not follow me in; he's abandoned me too. I run until I reach the clearing and the altar. This is it. This is the place I was supposed to be as the Spring Maid, and this is the place I ended up at still.

The painful rhythm in my chest is the cadence I chant to, saying over and over, "I will not submit, I will not submit. I am my own."

I place my hands upon the altar with its old blood stains and laugh through ragged breaths. I made it. I am free. No drugs, no seeds. Closing my eyes, I try to slow my breath and heart. If I had submitted and gone through with the ceremony, I would have been led here by the Elder and her acolytes, along with our chief and his warriors.

But not by my mother. She would have stayed back. My burdens are not hers to carry, but hers have always been mine to bear. Still, I love her unwillingly, but I cannot fight the fact that she is my mother. Maybe it's not her fault. Maybe I shouldn't blame her for being unable to love me because she couldn't see me as anything other than a Spring Maid. She was one after all, and I am the fruit that she bore from it. I am the reason she was allowed back into the village.

Maybe it's not fair for me to ask her to love something born through sacrifice. Although, I wish she would have seen me as her salvation. Is it wrong to love the pig meant for slaughter? Is it foolish of the pig to expect to be loved in return? I can't envision a life in which our relationship could have been another way, unless it was one in which a Spring Maid did not exist.

The black-haired woman in my dream has shown me more love than my own mother. I look around the altar and wish she would appear. I long to run to her as I did in my dreams, to wrap my arms around her slender figure, to tell her I did it. I am here. To have her arms return my embrace and match its strength and warmth and need.

To hear her call the name Berja, knowing it was meant for me, and have a mother in dreams be real.

Love never seems to be equal among parents and offspring. Not every child is loved or wanted, not every parent gets the child they expected. Is it better to be a child left out in the cold, to be taken away by the elements, or one to grow up without love? Watching always from the outside and wishing, dying, for what others have and they lack. What I lack.

I would never deny my child love or kindness. I would never hate them, hurt them, or send them off to their deaths for what they are or were born to be.

I am brought out of my musings by the rustling from the budding trees behind the altar. Near the stack of skulls from previous offerings, the branches with their budded leaves part and a giant, white, one-eyed bear comes through with a graceful lumber. Two ravens, black as night, fly above him, as if announcing his arrival just as a layer of mist on the forest floor unfurls before him. I take a deep breath and let it out, standing firm in my position by the altar between us. His big, blocky face leans over the hard stone slab of the altar and comes just inches from mine, his breath sweet and inviting.

The mist covers the giant white bear, obscuring him from my vision. I wait anxiously as the ravens above call out. The mist begins to dissipate, leaving a man with pale bare skin, strong bones and muscles, and larger than any man I have seen before, in the bear's place. It is as the dream mother had said.

"You are not filled with drink or seed," the man observes, though his lips do not move.

"No, I am not. I will not be," I say.

Pointing to my red-stained hands, he asks, "You have painted yourself like a warrior. Would you go to war then, for what you want? For what your heart desires?"

"I would fight," I answer. I know I am where I'm supposed to be.

"Then war it is," he states. My face burns with the sudden sting of his slap.

"Tell me what it is you want. Tell me what it is you will be fighting for," the man demands.

Tears threaten to spill from my eyes, but I refuse to show him that I'm surprised, that I am wounded. The woman from my dream had said he would give me a choice, but she did not mention that I would have to suffer for it. I take a deep breath and for a moment I consider running, but I am dead either way, so I might as well fight.

I steady myself before facing him and saying calmly, "I am fighting for myself. To be in control of my own life. To love. I want to care and be cared for."

I climb up over the cold stone altar, jumping down from it and boldly squaring my shoulders. I ball my fists and stand as tall and strong as I can. I am ready to fight.

"I cannot offer you that," he finally replies.

His one eye stares into both of mine and questions my resolve.

"Give me knowledge then, as you did my ancestors. You led them from the cave and now I ask you to lead me from my destiny as a Spring Maid. Give me the knowledge to create my own path, to create my own love, my own family. I would surely do better than those before me."

"I gave my eye for knowledge. What are you willing to give for your freedom? For something to love and be loved in return?"

"I have nothing to give up, only myself and my blood."

"That is enough. From that will come more," he says. "I can offer you something else to love and care for. I can offer you power, glory, but it must be earned. Are you willing to fight for it? Do you have the strength to take what you desire from me?"

I grab his throat with my hand and am quickly met with the stinging pain from his hand connecting with my cheek. My hand involuntary leaves his throat and covers my cheek. My eyes well with tears, but I will not allow them to fall. I stand before him again, tall and proud. I once again grab his throat and begin to mirror and match his movements. Hand for hand, clawing and biting, yielding and unyielding in a match of will, resistance, and power. There is no blow he can land that will make me quit. That will make me give up the new path before me that is just steps away.

"What is it that you want?" I ask through gritted teeth as I get up once more from the ground, a large rock in my bloodied hand.

His eye grows dark, and his voice turns into a growl as he charges me. "Warriors like no other to fill my hall and fight at the end with me."

I grip the rock and swing with all the strength I have left, connecting it with his one good eye. When it is over, I rest against the altar and look at his still body lying on the ground in front of me. No pain can outweigh the power of knowing that I have won.

"What did you fight for?" I ask the god as he opens his eye and picks himself up off the forest ground as if nothing had happened.

His body no longer shows any sign of the struggle between us. I watch him in awe, knowing he is truly a Forest God.

"I thought of the end and the battle that is ahead—a battle you will help me win. You will be the mother of great warriors who will love you, who will worship you. You will never be alone or unprotected. You will take pride in their glory and bask in their victories."

He leans forward and whispers in my ear the knowledge of runes, of hamr, hammrammr, the ability to change my form as he did. He warns me of the danger should I forget his wisdom. Should I read or speak the runes incorrectly. Grabbing my wrist, he kisses it, and the runes appear as burning, bright red scars that begin to slowly fade to light pink, then white.

With those last words, he steps back, and a golden apple falls from one of the ravens above. The Forest God catches the apple and places it on the altar declaring, "Your children will rise and call you blessed. Make sure they are worthy as I have made sure that you are."

He kisses my wrist one last time before changing once again into a giant bear and lumbering off as the ravens fly ahead of him, singing farewell. The mist once more swallows him up before dissipating and leaving me alone.

Grabbing the apple and marveling at its perfection, I climb back on to the altar and lay down, allowing the coolness of the stone to calm the fire that still burns inside me. I place my one arm by my side, palm facing the sky, gripping the smooth apple in my other hand as I repeat the words of the Forest God in my head over and over.

I bring the fruit to my lips and take a bite out of its firm, crisp skin, and then another and another. I suck in the sweet and tart juices from the fruit—the taste unlike any fruit I've ever had before—and stare at the sky as I finish the gift he had left me.

Feeling refreshed and renewed, I speak the words he had whispered to me, the ones that make the runes burn and glow upon my wrist. I repeat them as my body buzzes and I feel myself change. Fur grows upon my skin, my bones and muscle stretch and grow in a painful but also pleasing way. My teeth turn sharp and powerful, despite the aching from my mouth stretching to house them.

I feel alive and indestructible as I run around the clearing and into the forest, swatting and knocking down trees and throwing large rocks. Power courses through me as I bask in the freedom to play and test my new strength. Suddenly, my stomach flips and I return to my human form, throwing up at the base of a broken tree I had felled.

Exhausted from the changes to my body, I slowly walk back to my altar, now naked as the runes fade, to lay upon it and rest. My eyes grow heavier, and I hear the woman from my dreams call out to me, but the distant laughter of Little Bird hides her words and their meaning. I am too tired to care, too tired to do anything but sleep on my cold, hard bed. At first, I dream of nothing. Just empty darkness, which is neither filled with sound nor feeling.

A man's voice interrupts the endless void, telling me that I will stand upon the bank of a perpetual mist-filled shore. As he speaks, the darkness transforms. Coldness creeps in, filling the empty spaces around me. Shades of greys, browns, and blues begin to take shape until I feel the smooth pebbles and sea-beaten rocks under my feet. The gentle coolness of the water, lapping and pulling ever so lightly at the bottom of my dress.

I look toward the dark sky first, watching as the clouds and mist battle for form in front of a dim sun that they have kept veiled. The voice whispers to me again, telling me that I will wait here, waiting for those I love to return from a battle. I look to the sea and its gentle waves become turbulent, violent, and painfully cold. The waves swell and come to devour me. His voice is no longer a whisper, but loud as thunder as lightning fills the sky.

Berja

He says it is a battle they are destined to lose. The last crack of lightning, that last boom of thunder comes from the sound of my heart breaking.

Chapter
5

I am Berja

When I wake, my body feels as though it has been battered from the storm in the dream, but I know it is from my battle with the Forest God. I wipe away the icy tears that have worn a painful path down the sides of my face.

I look up expecting to still see the grayness of my dreams, but the sun is shining brightly through the gaps of the leaves instead—leaves that have started to unfurl from the morning heat. The wind blows gently but I shiver not from it, but from the memory of my dream.

I look around and feel disoriented. The warmth from the sun feels stronger against my skin. The leaves were just buds when I came here, and I know that some time must have passed since I fell asleep.

My stomach aches, and I know that I need food. Shaking off the bad dream, I focus on the now and listen to the forest. I sniff the air to try and discern the different scents from one another. The smell of garlic brings me to the green shoots of leeks and ramps sprouting from the ground. I begin to dig slowly into the firm soil, and the earth pushes into the spaces underneath my nails. The garlicky smell becomes stronger, and I dig faster until I have freed the small white bulbs from the earth. I eat them greedily, not bothering to shake off the clumps of dirt that still cling to them. I look around as I chew, spotting mushrooms on the tree trunks nearby. They're in the shape of the shells the men sometimes bring back from long trips. I eat those next. Still hungry, I head to the river to see what else I can find.

It's the end of the day by the time I have filled my belly with enough food to make the pangs of hunger go away. The moon is peaking out, but not quite full yet. I know I'm supposed to wait until the moon completes its full cycle, but there is no need. I am no longer a Spring Maid. I am Berja. I am powerful. I will be the mother of great warriors. I will be a mother. A better one than my own or the mother before her. My children will be strong and fierce. They will be free and they will be loved.

I will keep them safe.

The laughing of my green-eyed friend startles me, and I look up to see him resting on a branch above me.

"What is it that makes you laugh, Little Bird?" I ask.

"You think you have gained power, but you are still a Spring Maid. You have gained nothing from the Forest God. He has fooled you," the bird responds.

"My name is Berja, not Spring Maid. Tell me how there is no power in that? It is proof that I have power now. Something I can share if I choose. No more waiting, no more sacrifice. I can do what I want, what pleases me."

"You are still nothing more than a vessel to make more sacrifices for the benefit of others, Spring Maid. Your worth is still tied to the service and benefit of others."

"My children will be warriors, not sacrifices."

"What are warriors but servants and sacrifices to war?" He laughs again, and I shudder at the memory of my dream.

I hit the tree as hard as I can, causing it to shake and Little Bird to fly off. My knuckles yell at me in anger from the pain and my face burns hot from the bird's cackle.

"We are not at war now, and even if so, no man can match my strength or that which I will give my children," I declare.

"You are strong now, it is true. But the South Men will quickly take what is yours unless you take what is theirs first. You needn't wait to make an army, Spring Maid. You've seen the power you already yield. Go to the South Men villages and remind them why they fear the woods. Secure your domain before you lose it."

He's wrong, my green-eyed friend, my little bird. I am free, but only just so, and I can free the other Spring Children. I can free Eemil. No more days serving the Elder, waiting to be sacrificed to appease the spirits in the woods. Eemil can be free to join the men in the village—to hunt, to fight, to be a protector. He can lead a council with the Elder; one that can make decisions for the village. One that will continue to protect us against the South Men. With my gifts, I will change our future. No more waiting on a Spring Maid sacrifice to mark the start of the hunt and harvest. The forest is ours now—always. The South Men encroach at times, it's true, but they still fear the woods, and in time they will fear us too."

"I need to go to the village and free the Spring Maids first. Then, if need be, I will take care of the South Men," I say out loud, affirming my mission.

"You waste time instead of doing it now. You needn't wait for the creation of warriors—you are a warrior, Spring Maid," he laughs before flying off.

I sniff the air and find my way back through the trees to the altar path, but there is a sourness all around me. The bird continues to laugh in the distance, and I shake my head to remove the seeds of doubt he has planted. I won't let the words of my friend bring me to anger or undue action. I will heed the warning from my dream. I will make sure my children are not sacrifices to war. I won my gift from the Forest God, rightfully so.

I am the end of the Spring Maids.

I take a breath, and then another to calm my nerves and prepare myself for what is to come. For everything that I will do, that I will change.

Chapter
6
Not the Last

Through the forest, I reach the altar, and I learn that I was wrong.

I am not the last Spring Maid, and a heaviness falls upon me. My replacement lays cold upon the altar, his heart and blood collected days ago for the fields.

The Spring Child is younger than me, and if his eyes were not covered with cloth, they would be looking through the tree canopy at a moon that had already completed its cycle and started anew.

I take a deep breath, releasing it slowly with my sorrow and shame. I slept for too long, waited too long, and the cycle continued without me.

I will not leave him here, this boy. I will not let his skull be placed on top of the growing pile of nameless bones by the altar. I will not leave any of them on display anymore. I rest for a moment on my hands and knees in front of the blood-stained stone, allowing tears to flow freely down my face as I have never been allowed to.

I begin to dig.

When I first press my fingers into the ground, it fights me and refuses to open to me. I whisper the words of the Forest God and I feel the runes burn upon my wrists as I continue to dig. The pain grows as my hands change, but soon my large paws make quick work of the grave I design. With a large enough hole in the ground, I gently grab the Spring Child and drag him into the earth. He is followed by the collection of skulls the elders had amassed by the altar. When it is done, and they are covered safely in the earth, I transform back into my human form and lay upon the site where they are buried and close my eyes.

Can I really change this?

I cannot rest here.

I cannot allow the cycle of Spring Maids and Children to continue.

I pick myself up and give the altar one last look before turning back to the small dirt path that leads to the village. I take another breath in, and I focus on the damp, woody scents of the forest, on my new power, and how the earth doesn't feel as cold as it did when I arrived. I repeat the words given to me and transform once again into my bear form—what is beginning to feel like my true form—and listen. The forest, a place I thought was so eerily quiet, is deafeningly loud with life.

I walk down the winding path, one I used to fear but now control, until I come to the village entrance. I stop at the path's end and take in the sounds and scents of the village. It surprises and scares me.

Overwhelming is the unpleasantness of the smell of sickness. All around, I can hear sadness and worry. We are not as far from the life our ancestors had lived in the caves as the Elders led us to believe. The scent of death lingers, and I realize this must be what they have been hiding from us. This must be why they were so set to sacrifice us. I know in this moment that I can save them as I was intended to do. Not for a season, but forever.

I only knew my suffering; I never saw the full extent of it. But now I do. I know I can save them all if I choose. I can make them great warriors like the Forest God said, my warriors, if they deserve it. Thinking of the Spring Children before me, of the boy I had just buried, I am not sure yet that all the villagers do.

I take a few steps further into the village until I am finally noticed. I hear the calls and the fear and awe as more and more gather to take in the sight of me in my glory. My beautiful dark fur, my tall, heavy-boned frame, along with my formidable jaw filled with sharp teeth. I think in this moment how easily I could kill them. I can feel their blood running wet down my fur, their soft flesh between my teeth and claws. It makes me smile at first, then ashamed, and I push the thought away.

The men come with their axes and spears. The ceremony is over, and they are free to hunt me and other bears—the start of the season is upon us. I can hear their hearts beating in a wild frenzy. They look so small now, so weak, so different than when they surrounded me in my nest. It feels like that was only yesterday. Time has no place in my heart now that I have been gifted the power of gods.

I stand upon my two legs, let out a low growl, and transform back into my human form. I stand in naked perfection before them. The metals sing to me as weapons hit the ground, followed by some villagers who fall to their knees. Men who I once considered the village's mightiest warriors are amongst those on their knees.

There is a change in the way they look at me now. It is different from when I was just a Spring Maid held prisoner in the nest and it fills me again with the delicious taste of power. I am something to take notice of, something to be feared, something to be revered.

I look for him in the crowd of faces. The hard, compacted earth of the village paths feel unnatural compared to the ones in the forest but I ignore the distraction, continuing to search until I find my Eemil. I will not stop until I find him, a first child of spring, the man who will be my mate. More and more of them fall as they see me, on their knees like I am a living altar. I am a Forest God now. I am their salvation that they will sacrifice for.

I find him working in the garden, sweat making his muscular body glisten despite the cool spring air as he breaks open the ground in an empty field, preparing it to seed. As the others around him drop, he remains standing. I know something in him recognizes me, though I am taller, larger, and more beautiful than I was before. I can't be touched by anyone here except him because I choose to. I feel a hunger inside me grow as it did with the Forest God, and it is intoxicating.

I continue to take slow steps, savoring this new feeling. Savoring the power as it pulses inside me along with my heartbeat. I make my way to him and the struggle between control and giving into my power is thrilling, seductive. For so long I was denied the ability to feel anything but longing. For so long my soul has ached for his, and now he will be mine.

Standing before him, I listen to his pulse quicken and his heart race. I reach up, feeling his coarse hair between my fingers as I caress his face, then grab it firmly and bring his ear to my lips. I will set his body aflame along with mine. I will take what is mine. I will free him as I did myself, and we will be together in the new world I create for us. I will make him a god along with me because I know he is worthy.

It's just us, Eemil and I. The village fades as the pounding of our hearts synchronize.

"I am Berja," I tell him. "Tell me what you desire." But he just stares at me.

"I have been blessed, and am destined to be the mother of great warriors. I have the power to bestow upon you the same gifts if you are worthy. Tell me what it is you desire," I ask again.

"What does it mean to be worthy? What does that cost? I have only blood to give, and it does not belong to me, but to the Gods," he answers.

My face prickles at the truth of his words and tears threaten to show him the wound he created. That is the truth of Spring Children, of Spring Maids. That *was* the truth. It will not be any longer. Fire replaces the pain inside me.

"You have more than just blood. You can earn the gift from me. Fight me as the great bears do, and let's see whose will is stronger. Let us see who will submit." I cannot hide my smile or excitement as I utter these words to him. "Tell me what you desire. What is it you pray to the Forest Gods for?"

"To be a warrior. To be named. To take my place amongst the strongest of the men in this village." He drops the tool he was using to break open the earth.

His lips and hands return the force of mine before I push him back. I see the hunger in his eyes matching mine and know he accepts my offer.

"Follow me to the nest. Show me there what a good warrior you can be. Let us see if you sprout wings and fly from the nest as well as I did," I tease.

He is clever. I know he can sense my desire and seeks to distract me because he drops the cloth from his waist to the ground and meets me as I am. He catches me looking, and a smile grows across his face.

Eemil follows me to the nest, and a crowd of villagers and the Elder follow us, as well. The fresh flowers that had been laced into its branches have nearly dried out, but they still give off a pleasant fragrance around us. I had left this as a Spring Maid, and I returned to it a god.

I am surprised when he climbs into it before me with no hesitation and no fear. We circle each other, both predator and prey, within the confines of the nest. Rushing forward, I knock him down with a hard shove. I laugh when I hear him gasp, but my delight is cut short as he sweeps his legs under mine, catching me by surprise, and I fall. For a brief moment, we stare at each other, then scramble quickly to pin the other down. Wrestling turns into something more as we both fight to dominate the other, to see who can make the other submit first.

Our bodies begin to follow their own commands. I always knew he was worthy, had known in my heart he had won this battle before it even began, and my quivering body agrees. I whisper in his ear his prize, the words of the Forest God, which transform him as they did me. The runes on my body glow, and new ones appear on him, matching my own.

Something inside me loses control then. I embrace and become the primal feelings that course through me. We consume each other like the hungry beasts we are. For the first time, it is not me against destiny, it is us.

Too quickly does this moment pass. When it's over, I pull him up along with me and I see him taking it in——the new senses, the new power. We are no longer sacrifices. No longer servants. We are the start of our own people. We are each other's.

"You are Eemil." I say, then leave one last kiss upon his temple.

Chapter
7
Home

I am no longer alone.

For the first time, I have someone. I have love.

I stand up in the nest and turn to look at the silent faces staring at us—faces that had faded into a different world while I consummated with Eemil. I feel nothing for them as they stare; some in wonder, some in fear. I don't know what I expected coming back. Perhaps that after this change I would feel more like I belonged here, but I don't, and sadness begins to fill my belly.

"Come," I say, fighting to mask the emotions that have become harder to control as I take Eemil's hand and pull him behind me to leave the nest.

He says nothing. He doesn't move with me, but rather stretches his free hand and flexes as the power courses within him.

"To the woods," I order, pulling harder, but still he doesn't budge.

"Long have I dreamed of being a man of this village. Of being a hunter and a warrior like my father. I know they say the Spring Children are fathered by the forest, but I always knew whose seed I had come from. One cannot deny our connection by looks. Now you have given me power. You have given me a name."

It's true what he says. I too have heard the whispers of how he could be the twin of the village's greatest hunter—a man who is our greatest protector from any of the South Men who have thought to stray into our village path.

"What has happened to me?" Eemil asks and looks down upon me. "Is this a dream, a trick? Am I free now?"

"I have blessed you with the same gifts I have been given. You are not free to be a great warrior, you *are* a great warrior. Together we will make more—our own children. No one will ever be stronger than you, than us, than those that we create. You are free to hunt as you please. You are free to protect us, our family."

I grab his hand and place it upon my stomach as a promise to our future.

"What about them?" he asks, glancing toward the crowd of villagers that still stare at us.

"We are the start of our own family," I say, pushing his hand harder into my stomach. "A *real* family. We are of Spring Maids. They are not our family, but our keepers. I see even more now that there is nothing here but sickness and death. I am Berja. I am the mother of great warriors, starting with you," I boldly state before leaning in to kiss him.

"Berja, great mother, with these gifts you have brought back, we could be more. They could be more." He points to the crowd of villagers, Spring Children, and the elder. "We could put an end to the Spring Maids and Spring Children. We could protect our hunting and fishing grounds. I could lead the men as my father has done, in providing for the village, in protecting what's ours from the South Men who take and murder. No more hunger, no more sickness. No more endless days of tending the gardens and burying the dead. We could be the strongest people in this land, and no one would challenge us or take from us again. Surely this is what the Forest God wanted when he blessed you and sent you back to us," Eemil finishes, tone low and pleading.

His heart is softer than mine, but his wanting and desire are just as strong. We both have felt the emptiness of not belonging, of being forbidden to touch, to speak freely, to act as others were allowed to. Where I had desired and longed for a family, he has longed to be a great man of the village, a hunter, a protector, and to be recognized as such. He doesn't hold it against them for what they did to us, for what they kept from us. He sees only what could be.

But I also know what the Forest God wanted: warriors. Little Bird had said a warrior is just a sacrifice to war, and I can't help but fear he is right. I will not let my love or my children be sacrifices anymore for anyone, not even the Forest God who blessed me. I will keep them away from war, from battles they are destined to lose.

The forest calls, and I want to go back. The smells and sounds of the village that I am now open to are overwhelming and I want to retreat. My green-eyed friend is perched again on the holly tree watching me, cocking his head to the side, curious to see what my decision will be. I will prove my dear friend wrong, show him I did not make a mistake when I took the Forest God's offer. I won my gift, and I am not beholden to the god's desire. My children will be great warriors, but they will never see a day of war.

I drop Eemil's hand and leave him in the nest as I walk over to the holly branch. I sit down on the cold, damp ground, trying to drown out the deafening noises of their heartbeats and smell of their fear. My friend begins to laugh, and I growl in annoyance. From above, I am pelted with small, hard yellow and red berries that bounce off my head and land in front of me. Playfully, he laughs again as I stand up and swat the tree.

"Why do you fret so, Spring Maid? The village is yours now. Do with it what you will, what you desire. Burn it down to the ground if you choose. Show me you are not a tool or a sacrifice. Show me how you are the one in control now."

He takes one look at me with a gaze that sparkles with mischief and flies from the holly branch to the roof of the meeting hut. He flaps his wings and caws, looking down at them and me. I believe he would sing and dance upon their graves if I did as he suggests.

I get up and walk back to my nest. Eemil has climbed out and is surrounded by the villagers who marvel at his transformation. My mate is basking in the attention of the village men—he has never looked happier, more alive. I wish my attention would be enough for him, but I know how intoxicating it is to be seen by many after spending a life as the shadow to those who stand in the light. If I burned it all down, I would only be hurting him.

"Move this to the meeting hut," I command, interrupting the men. These were once the same men who encircled me like I was their prey, but they obey without hesitation.

Everything in this village is mine now if I choose. Is that what I want? I had always wanted to belong, but they never let me. But it is I who makes the decisions now. It is I who is in power. I can make them mine as they had made me theirs.

If I give them the rune magic, then they will be a part of me, we will no longer be separated. We will all be connected and a family. They could all be my children, and I could love and be loved, but it's not easy to love those who have refused to love you before. It is not easy to forgive and let go of the anger.

"You could also kill them all. It would be so easy," the Little Bird calls from the roof.

He echoes the thought I had pushed away when I first entered the village. Looking at them and their weak, small bodies, I know that I could, but what would I be left with besides blood and ruin? The longing and loneliness would remain long after the joy of that moment of reckoning had passed. I would be a monster.

The woman from my dreams had warned that they would call me that if I wasn't careful. I am not a monster, though. I will be careful with my words, knowledge, and desires. I will be careful with my actions. I will not act out of anger. I still want to love. To prove that I am capable of it.

That I am better than them.

As they move the nest, which is now my bed, I leave the village and head back to the altar of the Forest God. I know in my bones that our encounter was to be the only one—the Forest Gods are like that.

The path I once ran to escape I now walk to for refuge. The ground is just a little softer, a little warmer, and it gives way to me differently than it did before. I reach the altar and lay down upon its hard stone surface as the world spins, and I wonder how I can still feel so much emptiness. I have my lover, and I will have a child—I will have many, the Forest God promised.

I gaze up at the opening in the tree canopy and watch the sky for a while, getting lost in the peaks of blue amongst the greens, when I hear the small squeak and rustle down below. Sitting up, I see a girl—not much younger than myself—kneeling before the altar, before me. The same dark hair, the same bright blue eyes—she could be my sister had we not been born Spring Children.

"Why have you come here?" I ask.

"Spring Maid."

"No," I correct her, "Berja. Who are you?"

"I am a Spring Child like you were once," she replies.

"What is your name?"

"Spring Child."

"No, what do you call yourself?"

She looks at me puzzled and answers, "Spring Child?"

Anger rises quickly in me. I have had to hide my emotions all my life, and now that I am able to set them free, I struggle with letting them out. It pains me, and the words in my head scream out, '*Never again.*'

"What do you want?" I slide off the altar and come to stand before her. Up close, I can see she is a brave one—not one to surrender.

"I want to be like you. No longer a sacrifice, but something more, something free."

"What are you willing to sacrifice for freedom and love?"

"Everything," she replies.

The girl takes a knife from the folds of her clothes and holds it to her neck.

I grab her face in my hand and place a kiss on her lips as I take the knife from her. I move my lips to her ear and say, "Not with blood. Submit your will to me and you will be my daughter."

"No," she says and pulls away from me. "If I am your daughter, then I cannot submit. Submission is the old way, the way of the Spring Children and Maids. You are bringing us to the new way, to your way. I heard you bless him. I wish to be like you and like Eemil. I want to be brave, to be a warrior. I will fight to prove my worth, to show that I am worthy."

She steps further away and puts herself into a defensive stance. "I will not submit."

I smile at her boldness. I walk around her slowly as she holds her stance. Her frame is thin and underfed, but my gift will change that. Her heart beats in excitement and as I transform into my bear form. I am pleased that she does not run in fear.

I walk closer to her until my large head is almost touching her face, yet she still does not tremble. I open my large mouth only to lick her, sending her into a fit of laughter as I gently knock her to the ground with my large forearm. I transform back into my human form, scooping her into my arms and repeating the words of runes as I cradle her like a babe. I feel their power course through me and into her. The girl gasps, breathless from the power that surges through her tiny limbs. I feel more fulfilled as the runes appear lightly on her skin just below her ear. The empty spaces inside me begin to fill, and I think this must be what happiness and love feels like.

"Your name is Enni," I tell her, kissing her lightly upon her dark head.

"Mother," she says, "my duty is now to you. Thank you for this blessing."

I know this must be love. This must be belonging. And this is power. I look at her sweet face, this Spring Child who is now my daughter, now a Forest God like me. I know now what I am missing, what the Forest God meant.

I must make my own people, my own village. I will take the Spring Maids and Spring Children and make them my own. I will be their mother, and they will be my children and love me.

I take my daughter's hand, and we transform together into our bear form and romp and run through the trees. We make a game out of the light that shines down in the gaps of the trees, jumping from one spot to the next. We splash in the nearby river, and for the first time in our lives, we have fun and play as a family. When we have played to our heart's content, we both turn back into our human form and I lead her, my first daughter, back to the village.

As we walk the path back, I can't help but notice that the trees seem a little fuller, a little greener. The earth and sun feel a little bit warmer and softer. We enter the center of the village, and I see the villagers stop and look at her, noticing her new power and status next to mine.

"Go. Go and fetch all the Spring Maids and Children. Look into their eyes and when you recognize that desire to be free—the same desire that burned in you—bring them to me one by one so that I may grow our family and our freedom."

She kisses my hand and tells me, "Yes, Mother."

As she runs to carry out her task, I see that she is a little bit fuller, less frail. She will only continue to grow in strength and power.

With Enni off to collect the Spring Children, I retire back to my nest at the meeting house and wait. I climb within the safety of its walls and sink into the dried bedding that still smells lightly of Eemil. I look up at the ceiling and think of how I will have my children gather fresh herbs and branches to hang from the rafters. If I cannot live in the forest, then I will bring the forest into my home. We will make this like a cave fit for a Forest God, a mother bear.

I move my hand absently and am met with something I had forgotten about. My little doll, the one Little Bird and I had made together. She brings with her an unpleasant sensation in my stomach and head. She wears the old stains of the berries from the day I left, and her body and arm have been broken from my fight with Eemil.

Berja

She had been the thing I had wished upon—a symbol of my deepest desires. Now, she is just the broken husk of an old life that I will not return to. She is a symbol of my weakness, of my loneliness, and I fear that if I do not destroy her then those things I left behind will return to me once more. I hold her in my hand as I climb out of my nest and to the hearth in the back of the room and toss her into the fire. She burns and takes with her the pain of the past.

Never again is the promise I make.

Chapter
8
My Children

Berja

It's not long before Enni returns and lets me know she has gathered the Spring Children. Over the next nine days, I bring them in one by one and ask those who are old enough to respond to the same questions. Who are they, who do they want to be, will they submit. The Spring Children vary in age from yearlings to men and women older than my mother. Those are the ones who have been spared thanks to the successful seeding and return of a Spring Maid. I kiss them and name them, and my children grow from one to twenty-seven.

With each new Spring Child transformed, I feel my own power grow, and with it so does a hunger for more. The life I had dreamed of becomes closer and closer to being reality. This is our house now, I tell them. No need to be separated any longer. No need to be held apart. They are free to love and be loved. They are mine now after all, and they can love something that belongs, that is theirs.

"Enni, have the men build a larger house for the younger children. They should live among their own kind now. Among those who will love them." Enni nods and leaves to carry out her task.

"Berja," my mother's voice rings out as she approaches me, cautiously at first.

She is met by a chorus of low growls by some of my children, which both surprises and pleases me. They are in tune with me, my children. Again I think how this must be love, and I crave it more and more.

I say nothing to the woman who bore me as she continues to walk undeterred to me. I wait for her to come closer. I can smell her,

~ 55 ~

but there is no fear in her scent—it is something else. Her heart should be beating fast like the others, but it is frustratingly calm.

"They say you are gathering the Spring Maids and Spring Children," Mother calls. "Bestowing your gift from the Forest God upon them, by his order. I am both, am I not? I am here for my gift from the Father."

"Not the Father," I say. "From me."

"Berja, you did not create this yourself; we all know that. It was given to you, and it is your duty to give it to us now, to me."

I turn from her to walk away, and she places her hand on my shoulder, something I have always longed for. Maybe this is how I make her see, maybe this is how I connect her to me and show her that she can love me.

"Leave," I command her.

I am the one in charge now.

"Yes, Mother," she says back to me, and the hair on my skin stands up and my blood turns cold.

She kisses my hand and walks away obediently. The world around me spins, and my heart races. I fall into my nest, my back against its bottom and look up at the spinning ceiling. Mother? A flutter of wings and a caw from my Little Bird brings me back. His two bright green eyes peer into mine as he flaps his wings in my face, telling me that's enough, to snap out of it, and he's right. I push myself into a sitting position and he flies away, his laughter never far from my ears.

My mother was a Spring Maid, but I have no intention of sharing the gift with her. She is no Spring Maid now, just another villager. As I gather my wits and strength, Enni comes in with Erikka, one of the Spring Maids I had given the gift to, and I recognize her as the one who had mouthed at me to run the day I earned my power. It seems so long ago now.

"What is it?" I ask.

There is no shyness in Erikka—she would have never made it through the ceremony—and I am glad for her that I have ended the practice. She looks me in the face boldly before kneeling and saying, "Mother, you have told us to go and be free in our love. But the love I have chosen is not of a Spring Maid line. He is not gifted, but he is strong and kind."

"What is it you are asking of me, child?"

Erikka now stands and asks, "Please, share your gift with him so that we may be together as equals. That we may bear our own children in our image and not that of those who would have sacrificed us. Please, Mother, I beg of you."

"I never said you could not be with the villagers," I reply.

"But Mother," Erikka begins again, "I want him to be as me. So that we can roam the forest together and he can see the world now as I do, experience it as I do. So that our children will be as me and not as a villager. When a horse is bred with a donkey, the offspring is sterile. Do you not see that it will be the same with us? I want my child to be strong like me. I do not want to risk my baby being like the villagers are, as we were before you gave us new life. Weak, unable to change their predetermined destiny like we were before you. I do not want my children to suffer the past as their future. Please, Mother," she begs.

I can see her pain and feel her desire and desperation. It was once the same as mine, the same feelings I had had for Eemil. If I deny her, then I am no better than the elders who controlled our fate—those who determined we were not to be allowed love. I am better than the elders. I am better than the mothers who bore us.

"Bring him to me now," I say. I will not deny my children the chance to love.

"Enni, stay with me."

She nods, and Erikka rushes to give me a big hug and kiss before running out. My blood heats and my heart warms, and I crave that affection and mourn the ending of the embrace. So, this is what it feels like to be loved. This is what it feels like to be a real mother. I know now that what I had been saying to myself—that I would do anything for my children—was true. That my mother was wrong. That I am capable of love, of great love, but I do not like that I am forced to bless the villagers. They have not earned the right as we have. I cannot bless them the same way I blessed my children.

"Will it work?" Enni asks, interrupting my thoughts.

"It will work," I tell her. "But they cannot be blessed the same way you were. They are not Spring Children."

"Maybe we should give them the drink that the Spring Maids were given. It is known to help with transformation. The Elder says it opens one's soul up. It prepares one's body for the Forest Gods' blessings."

I nod my head and agree.

"Go gather the herbs and let my other children know that if they too want to choose a villager to join them as their mates to bring them to me tonight. But only mates, no one else. Do not tell the rest of the village anything, especially my mother."

Enni nods and goes to begin her work. I hear my green-eyed friend laughing in the rafters, and I know he thinks this is funny.

Maybe it is cruel of me, but it seems only fair that the villagers go through what Spring Maids have had to go through. If they are truly worthy, then they won't mind. If they are worthy, then they will survive. That is what they had told us, and now that is what we will tell them.

Erikka and Enni bring him in and are followed by the rest of my children who file in along the walls.

"Take off his clothes," I order.

"But Mother?" Erikka protests, blue eyes widening, but she falls silent when I hold up my hand.

"What is your name" I ask him.

"Tero," he responds.

"Enni, Erikka, help him into the nest. Do you know why you were brought here?" I ask.

When he doesn't reply, I answer for him, "My daughter has chosen you for her mate. She thinks you are worthy. Are you worthy of this bride?" I gesture at my daughter. He looks at Erikka, and I can tell he returns her affection.

"Yes," he says bravely.

"I was once told that there is no point in loving something that will never be yours. Errika chose to love you anyways."

"We were always each other's no matter what the Elders said." His words make my heart swell and tears threaten to spill, but I quickly push the feelings down.

"My children, will you accept Tero into our family? Step forward and place your hands upon him if so."

I see them all step forward and do so, and my smile grows. A power grows within me, and my body buzzes with divine life. I grab the cup that Enni had prepared and step forward into the nest where he now kneels within.

"Drekka," I say, smiling as he opens his mouth obediently and sips. There's something about being in this position, seeing it as an Elder would, that calls to a dark place in me. The Spring Children were gifted not by submission, but the villagers must submit to me for their blessing, just as they had made us submit to them.

Grabbing a handful of his hair and pulling his head back roughly, I place a kiss upon his mouth, then below his ear. I bite hard and whisper the words of the Forest God. No, I whisper the words of the Mother, of me. As I utter the last word, he begins to convulse and scream. Tero writhes and grunts as my hand remains upon his head, and the hands of my children hold him down.

I can hear the laughter of Little Bird, who watches up above with his mischievous gaze, and I laugh too at the violence of his change that is so different than that of mine and the Spring Children. It feels like justice. Perhaps this proves we were made to handle pain and the villagers were not. My children are calm, save for Erikka, who looks to me with pleading eyes as the man before us twists and his muscles begin to strain and veins bulge. Soon, his skin color changes, and hair begins to sprout. His mouth opens, and a fierce growl rings out before he finally bursts into his new form, that of a great brown bear.

He stands upon his hind legs and lets out a deafening roar and the room erupts in bursts of fur and a chorus. Erikka beams at me before changing herself and biting his neck to drag him out of the room to beckon him to run with her into the woods—to enjoy the new freedom and power of their form. The rest of my children follow, and a great ruckus begins of playful fighting and carefree romping, something that we were never allowed to do before.

My heart grows, and so does the power that courses within me. I have made myself a great and mighty family. We shall never know fear or servitude again. I laugh in the warm sunlight, because there is no greater joy than this, watching my family. I feel Eemil's hands slide over my body from behind and come to rest on my stomach. My stomach which will soon grow with a child taken freely and given out of love, not duty.

"They're all watching," he whispers into my ear, talking of the villagers.

I turn and see my mother who is watching with them.

"Let them watch," I declare.

"You were right. We should leave, find our own place. As our family grows, we outgrow this place," Eemil ponders.

But I look at the meeting house that holds my nest and my friend perched upon it. With the numbers of my children growing, this place now feels like it belongs to me.

"This is our home," I reply. "We control the village now. We will continue to shape it to our image."

I tell my husband and our children to bring the forest to our village, to gather the fallen branches in the forest and stones by the river. We will make our homes an extension of the woods.

Chapter
9

Seasons

The sun hangs longer in the sky as the days stretch on and late spring turns into summer. Our family grows with a few more mates selected from the villagers to be companions for my older children. My belly grows with the new life Eemil and I created together. As I walk the village soaking in the warmth of the long summer days, I see the first signs of some of my children's bellies beginning to swell with a new line of us to come.

The yearlings and younger children continue to grow, and it is at a quicker pace than before their blessing. The ruckus and mischief of these young cubs makes me laugh. I watch them, the first Spring Children free to play and laugh. The promise of the future I had wanted so badly has been fulfilled.

I have freed the Spring Children. I have ended that line and created my own.

Some of the villagers are accepting and joyful of our new line, while others remain wary. Some have joined with my mother and continue to ask to be allowed to join us, but they are not worthy, at least not yet, and so I continue to tell them no.

It is easy to forget about them, the villagers. They mean nothing to me now. Some of them still hold meaning for my children, and I should love what they love, but it is hard and does not come naturally.

I try to tell my children to turn more to the forest to sustain us, but they still hold onto the old ways and farm, fish, and hunt with the village. With our new powers comes a larger appetite, which has started to take its toll on the village's ability to grow and farm enough food. I can sense the worry, hear the murmurs from the villagers who then try to poison my children with their fears. If we are running out of food in the summer, how will we survive the winter, they say. I tell them the forest will provide for us, and to ignore the doubts of those who are not like us.

My baby will arrive after the snow has covered the ground. I tell them to go to the woods and continue to gather what they can. To forage, to hunt, to grow what we can. To push the boundaries of our range that we've grown out of.

The sunlight and long days that peaked in the summer have begun to shorten into the harvest months. I grow more tired as I wait out the arrival of my child in the nest amongst the youngest of the Spring Children who come to nap and snuggle with me. Eemil, Erikka, and Enni handle the running of the village and my children. They manage keeping us fed and ensuring peace amongst the villagers and us.

The colder air carries on it a smell of worry, and fear begins to grow. I try to ask Eemil what troubles him when he comes at night to sleep, but he tells me not to worry. I don't want to worry, I want to stay in my nest and rest, so I do. I soak in every touch, every sound from my new life, and I push away the scent of anxiousness coming from outside the walls of our manmade cave. As I doze in and out with the little ones, I hear scuffling outside and my mother comes bursting in.

"Mother!" she yells. "You cannot hide in here while we are attacked and our land stolen from us. How will you feed the new mouths you have created whose hunger is not easily satisfied? You call yourself the Mother, yet you do not act like one. I knew you were not capable of love.”

“I am not your mother, do not talk to me of love,” I snarl back.

“What are you doing, Mother? Outsiders are encroaching upon our land, making homesteads and hunting our game, taking our fish and the plants we forage. You told us to turn to the forest for more food, but the forest is being taken from us! We should attack them now with our great strength, but you refuse to allow us to use it!” she continues to yell at me.

“What are her words?” I ask Eemil. I see a line grow in his forward as he shoves her out, but she pushes back and refuses to leave.

“You are a mother now. You must fix this, or your children will die along with us.”

I growl a warning at her: *‘Get out.’* And she does.

“What does she mean?” I ask.

“What she speaks is true. There are homesteads popping up from the South Men, encroaching on the forest, and a large village has been built a few days’ walk away. They are claiming the land for themselves. They’ve put up traps in the woods and we have had a few close calls with the children being ensnared in them. I will take care of it, of them. I am the protector of our family, of this village.”

The guilt hits me, and the truth that I have neglected my other children while selfishly enjoying my upcoming first birth slaps me with a cold sting.

"The South Men have always been afraid of our forest. Has anyone been hurt?"

"Not yet," Eemil answers, "But we should consider moving. South Men have grown braver. We are Forest Gods now—we can move to the cliffs, to the caves deep within the forest, from where our people first came."

"No," I reply. "You know what lives up there. I will not bring our people back to knowing only one season—that of death."

"That is just a story, Berja."

 No," I say.

"If we stay here, then we will need to fight," Eemil insists. "I am more than ready to do so, but you have been against it."

"We have strength, so we could. They are just human after all," I hear Erikka's voice say from behind us.

"Change the rest of us and we would be unstoppable. Remind them why they should fear the forest. Let their blood fill our rivers and soak our fields. Let them fear us." This time, it is my mother's voice that chimes in from outside the door.

"You would make us monsters," I remark. "No, the entire village is not worthy of the gift, not ready for it. Why would I give it to them when they were so uncaring for me and the others? They want the power, not the love and family that comes with it. Go, take some of the others with you and mark the trees with your claws, rub our scent amongst the trees. If they are smart, they and their dogs will get the hint. They will not stray into our part of the forest or encroach upon it anymore. They will see our signs and remember there are dangerous secrets the forest keeps."

"What about what they've already taken?"

"Let them have it. We will push further into the northern part of the woods. There is no reason for us to fear it now; we are part of it."

"What about the rest of us?" Mother asks.

"The rest of you are not my concern. Not my responsibility," I answer bitterly.

"I am a Spring Maid, your mother. I am your blood."

"That does not make you my family."

"We should not have to leave our home," Erikka interrupts.

"Erikka," Enni says gently, "don't you feel the forest call to you? We don't belong in houses with peat and moss roofs. We belong in the forest with our own kind. Maybe it's time we leave the village to be as its meant to be: a village of humans, not bears, not Forest Gods."

"No." Erikka is persistent. "My husband's family is still human. He will not leave them, and I will not leave him, not after I finally got a family. Not after I finally found my place and acceptance here. You say they are not your concern, but they are mine, and I am yours, am I not?"

Erikka storms off and I wish I didn't understand her feelings—how after years of longing and wishing to be loved and touched it is finally given. The idea of losing it drives you mad. You would do anything to ensure you never lost it.

Berja

"Where are you going to go?" I hear the cawing of my green-eyed friend and I ignore him. I will go to the altar to see if I can call the Forest God or the dream mother to me, to see if they have wisdom for me.

I kiss Eemil and head to the path alone. My little bird laughs as I turn to leave, and I see him flying over Erikka with his wide black wings. I should feel comforted, but I feel the tiny hairs on my arms rise up instead. There is a coldness in my stomach that I cannot shake.

I begin to walk down the forest path, shrouded with the changing leaves of the dying foliage—a symbol of the changing seasons. The further I go, the darker it becomes as the fullness of the trees become denser, blocking the sunlight entirely. It is not long before I reach my destination.

The altar with its smooth stone is always cool to my touch. My fingertips graze it lightly as I walk around it, listening, willing, and waiting for the Dream Mother to appear. She has only ever appeared in my dreams when I was still a Spring Maid, and I am much too awake and am far from that person I was. I climb upon the table of the altar and lay down as I did those many months ago. I feel my body try to sink into the unyielding stone and wait for slumber to take me.

Dreams cannot be forced, and the dream mother cannot be conjured. The longer I lay, the more awake I feel. I call for her in my mind, but she does not come.

I am alone.

Chapter
10

A Village
of
Monsters

When I return to the village, it is quiet—too quiet. It looks as though the village has been abandoned, but I can hear the rapid beating of hearts in distress coming from my nest. I run, panicked. Where are my children? Where is Eemil? I try to open the door, but it is stuck. The bear within me emerges and I knock it down and am met with Eemil in bear form who stands ready to strike before he realizes it is me.

I transform back and look around the room.

"What has happened?" I ask.

He looks away and goes back to the nest to where some of the children are being cradled by Enni.

"What has happened?" I demand and rush to them.

"It's Erikka," Enni answers, handing me one of the children to comfort. "She went with her mate down to confront the trespassers and he was killed. She flew into a rage and was injured as well and forced to flee. We went down with her, only to find they had skinned him—his bear hide was hanging out. We brought her back and, in her rage, she listened to your mother. She tried to use your rune magic to change your mother and the others into us."

"Did it work?" I ask, astounded, but a coldness fills my stomach.

"Yes and no. It's as if only their mind changed and became stuck in the rage and hunger, but not their bodies. Erikka took them down to the homesteads. We have not seen them since. Berja, we need to leave before they come back! They are not us anymore; they are feral and wild and dangerous. We are strong, but they outnumber us. We do not wish to kill them, as they were our family, but we do not wish to stay here with them anymore. Please, let us leave and find a new home far away from this wickedness," Enni pleads.

It is as the Dream Mother had warned. They would take my words and twist them, corrupt them in their grief, in their anger. It is as my mother had warned—love would lead me to fear and anger.

"I need to see for myself," I say, handing the child to Eemil. I leave them behind and head for the back of town, toward the woods where the homesteaders encroach.

The walk that should have taken a few days has only taken half of one. I did not realize they had come so close in the passing months. It's not long before I begin to smell the blood and signs of rot. Soon, I hear the feral snarls and munching of bones and flesh. When I arrive, I see the monsters. They still have some of the look of who they used to be, but now they crawl on all fours, their faces twist in scowls, and their movements are sharp, quick, and animalistic.

"Erikka?" I call out, but I do not see her.

I look into the home with blood-soaked walls and see my mother crouched underneath the skins of humans with a partially eaten head before her. She is licking the blood off the side of a face that is frozen in terror. Mother looks up at me and hands me something grey and squishy from inside the cavity, which turns my stomach. She laughs and quickly begins to eat that too. I run out of the house and lose my stomach at the sight and the smells accompanying it that overwhelm me.

It's then that I catch the sound of sobbing, and I make my way over and see Erikka on the ground, hunched over the skin of her dead lover. I hear the familiar laugh and catch my green-eyed friend watching the scene below him from a branch.

"Erikka," I say gently.

Her agony makes my heart break, despite the gruesome scene. The emotions of horror and grief fight for dominance, but in the end, she is my child, and her pain brings me sorrow over the monstrosity of what happened here. I reach out and touch her shoulder, but she flinches away.

"Erikka, what happened here?" I insist.

"They killed him, so we killed them. I made sure the man responsible would feel the pain I felt, of losing someone you love, of seeing their skin hanging. I made sure they all would feel my pain." Her words are cold.

"Erikka, there is another homestead not far from here. They will come at some point to see what has happened."

"We shouldn't keep them waiting." Erikka smears her face with blood as she wipes away her tears.

"Erikka, stop this."

"Stop this? Will you not avenge your child, Mother? Will you not fight for your children? They came onto our land. They killed one of us. They killed your child! You would do nothing? You would have your children do nothing?"

"These are not my children, Erikka. They are your creation. You should not have done what you did. You have started a war that all of us will have to fight."

"I am your child, am I not? You swore to love me? Or does only the child from your womb count now? Is that the only one you will fight for?" she says, pointing to my swollen stomach.

"Erikka, stop. I may not have borne you, but you are my child—I created you all the same. And you created them through me without my knowledge or permission. You have taken my words and corrupted them."

"Is the child of your child not yours then? Are you not blessed to be so fruitful?"

"These are monsters, Erikka. Look at them. They once sent us to the forest alone as sacrifices. You tried to give them something they were not worthy of, and it has turned them into the monsters they always were. Our true family lies in fear in the village, in fear of you and of them. It's not too late to come back with me, to come home with me. Leave them, Erikka. Leave them in the woods. Come home with me, to your real family. You have given the South Men a reason to fear the forest again. Let us hope they leave it at that and do not seek vengeance."

"No, Mother, we are still Spring Maids, just with more valuable hides. These intruders will continue to come and take those we love. What was the point in freeing us, in giving us hope and love, if we are just going to lose it?"

"Come back with me, Erikka, please," I beg.

I reach out to her, but my mother comes between us and snarls at me. She grabs Erikka's hand, and so do more of the creatures that come to surround her, snatching at her legs and arms. Their touch, so aggressive and strong, is blood-soaked.

"Please, Erikka, come home with me." I nearly choke on the words as a lump rises in my throat.

"You have become blind, Mother. The child in you has blinded you from your other children. I think it's time we save you from that burden and free you once again."

"Come near me and I will kill you all," I growl, my body buzzing.

"The truth is revealed. We were never your babies, though you call us your children. You are unfit to be our mother, unfit to lead us, to command us," my mother snarls from where she crouches, arms wrapped around Erikka. Each word comes from a voice I no longer recognize—throaty, broken, and inhuman. "Erikka is mother now."

"Erikka, please." I want to go to her, but I cannot. These creatures have built a barrier around her, and I can't get closer. As much as I plead with her, the whispers of the creatures drown me out.

Her pain is too great, and I cannot get to her. I cannot comfort her. I cannot make it better. What choice do I have but to leave without her?

I beg her to not do what they are planning next, to not wage this war—to not make me her enemy, but she is too far gone, and I must get back to the rest of our family and warn them. There is a hunger in these creatures. They will not stop, and we may be next.

"It is time for us to rise, for the world to see your blessings, Mother. This is just the beginning!" Erikka announces as I turn my back on her and the monsters she has created.

The walk back is uncomfortable, and it feels as though I am leaving behind a piece of me. Guilt and sorrow threaten to devour me, and I feel their grip as tight as the hands of the monsters who grasped my daughter. What kind of mother leaves behind her child, even one swallowed in darkness? The kind of mother that I swore I would never be.

And now I see it, the sacrifice of one for the sake of many. I see now why my mother had chosen to never love me, because it was to lessen her own pain. No, I would gladly take this pain in exchange for the gift of my daughter. I will not give up on her yet. I must find a way to free her from the dark path she has taken. To help her rid the monsters of her own creation.

I start to run, but I am alone. My green-eyed friend has abandoned me. Maybe he was right. Perhaps I should have confronted the South Men when I first received my gifts.

Maybe then I could have spared my daughter this agony.

Chapter

11

Mother of Monsters

Berja

The emotions are too much, and the child within me protests. I am forced to stop multiple times on the way back from the intensity of the cramping. The child will not wait. I am forced to search for someplace hidden in the woods, amongst the trees and freshly fallen leaves, and await the child. The sky grows dark, and I labor alone, calling out for a dream mother who never comes. I push and grunt through the pain for what must be hours. Sweat pours from my brow and I tremble from the intensity of it all. Shadows lurk beyond my reach and at times I feel that I am not alone.

Dawn breaks, and with it comes the first child born of my blood. There is no time for us to rest, to soak in this moment of joy. I do my best to stand up with my child and walk back to our family despite my pain and bleeding. My legs feel weak, my arms heavy, and the bundle of skin pressed to my chest is warm. It feels like much longer of a journey. I stop only to rest momentarily and kiss my child's head, but eventually we reach the outskirts of our village.

When I reach our house, I see that Eemil and some of the others have cautiously made their way out of the safety of my house and nest. The village looks as though it was torn apart by animals. Some of Erikka's children had beaten me home in the night. Eemil and the others had managed to scare them off, killing a few in the process. Their twisted bodies lay in a heap on the ground, their cursed blood staining the dirt.

"Berja," Eemil says with concern. "We can't stay here."

"We can, but we need all our children," I reply and show him the baby. "We need to get Erikka back from them."

"It's too late, Mother," Enni presses. "Her grief, her pain… it has turned her into the monsters she has created. We need to fight them or get far away from this place."

"To fight them is to fight Erikka. I do not care about the others, but some of my children might. Your mate might, as they are part of their family."

"Berja, if I may speak," says a woman from the village who is not one of us. She, along with a smaller band, had hidden with my family when they saw what was going on. "They are gone. Whatever words Erikka spoke to them, it changed them, twisted them. They are not who they were anymore. They are not who we once loved. The power you have, that you gave to your family, is more powerful than the monsters though. If you shared it with us, we could easily outpower them. We stand with you whether you share it or not though."

I look around at the remaining villagers who sought refuge with my family. I see they are mostly related to the villagers who were changed to be mates for my children, though some are not.

"Okay," I say quietly. Deep down, I know there is no other way. "Enni, there is no time for the drink. Let us do this and do it quickly. Let us pray we do it right. Anyone who looks like the monster Erikka has created, kill immediately."

One by one I go about changing them and by the end, the power that once felt so easy to call upon is hard to reach. Collapsing on the floor after the last villager has changed, I feel empty. I do not feel bonded to them as I do my other children. They do not call me mother. I am just their leader now, and they are my people. I weep at the loss of connection—there is nothing precious or miraculous about this anymore.

The young children and babies are gathered in the long house and placed safely in my nest while the adults spend the fall and winter months working to fortify the village. The days begin to stretch longer as the earth begins to awaken—the first spring any of us have seen without a Spring Maid and that sacrifice. I used to think monsters only came with the darkness, but now I see that they come in the light just the same.

Months stretch on and we have not heard or seen anything from Erikka or her creatures. It has been many months since I have seen my green-eyed friend, and only when I hear his laughter do I stand from where I was. I run out and look down the path that leads out of the village to see him riding upon the shoulder of a man dressed for battle. Eemil comes out and starts to growl.

"Stay calm," I urge, and I send the others a look as well.

"No one change, no one move," I say. I walk up to the man and tell him, "I know your friend. He was once mine, as well. Let us talk as friends. Tell me what it is you are here for."

The man looks at me, then past me to Eemil.

"Is this your village?" he asks Eemil.

"It is my village," I interject, a growl escaping my throat.

"A familiar sound we've been hearing in our woods, before our farms are attacked and our people slaughtered. Demons in the forest being led by a woman," the man replies with a raised brow.

Soon, the man is joined by eight others on large, heavy-boned horses. They line up just behind him, and I know that we can easily destroy them, but their swords are great, and I do not wish any harm to come to my children—those who I can still call mine.

"What do you want?" I press.

"I dreamed of this place once, and the voice of a man told me that I would find my glory here." He eyes the village with a wicked gleam.

"Are you waiting on an attack or planning to wage a war?" he asks, acknowledging our defenses.

"What do you want?" I repeat with a harsher tone. Forty-four of my children gather behind me. He whistles at a man behind him, who gets off his horse with a large bag dripping in what I can smell to be old blood. The man hands me the sack and I stare at him. He grins and drops it at my feet before stepping away.

"Go on then, open it. If you are a friend, then consider it a gift," he tells me, and the black bird upon his shoulder lets out a shriek-like laugh. I eye them, then look back at my family and cautiously undo the strings to find Erikka's dead eyes staring back at me.

A pain rips through me and I scream out in rage. So immense is the fury that I succumb to the runes and transform into the beast— the bear—that I am. I rush the man, and his horse rears back, as well as several of the horses behind them. I slash his horse's throat with my paw and send it to the ground. The man does not fear me, but rather draws his sword and swings as I duck and knock him with my paw. I feel the pain of an arrow in my shoulder and am soon surrounded by the men when I hear Enni call out to stop.

"Please!" she shouts. *"Please."*

The men do not give up their position, and I feel her hand upon me.

"She was her daughter, my sister, but we are not responsible for the others. They are not our family—they are not us. We built our defenses to protect ourselves from them," Enni pleads with them.

The threat has lessened. I grunt and slow my breathing. Erikka was my daughter, and no matter her actions, I will never see her differently. As the adrenaline dies, I transform back into my human shape and grit my teeth as I pull the arrow out slowly, keeping my eyes locked with the man as I do. Baring my teeth, I toss it at the man's feet.

"She looks like a monster to me. She acts like a monster," he whispers. Despite it all, it is clear he is in awe of such power. "If she was your kin, then you are responsible for her actions. A debt is owed."

"There is still a large group of the monsters that need to be killed—not one can be left alive. We are down men from an attack last night," another calls from his steed.

"You will give us your best fighters as payment for the lives we lost."

"No," I say and spit at the ground. The man holds his sword up toward my face.

"A debt is owed," he hisses.

Eemil steps between us, placing his hand on the man's sword and gently lowers it.

"I will go," he offers.

More of my children step forward and volunteer to go, as well.

"We can track them, and we can also help kill them if you leave our home alone. If you leave our mother alive."

"Only the men," the man says. "We've been warned about your women, and your mother has proven how unstable and dangerous they can be."

"No, Eemil." I grab his arm. "We are stronger than them. We can kill them all right now." As I let go of his arm and begin to growl, Eemil puts his arms around me and whispers in my ear.

"We could, but it is smarter to let them help us get rid of Erikka's demons than risk more of our own getting hurt."

Speaking loudly to the leader of the South Men, Eemil responds with, "Fine."

"No," I beg him. He is my mate, the man who has seen me through thick and thin. I cannot risk him or more of my children getting hurt.

"It's the only way." His words are calm, but his heart races.

I can sense that something here excites him, and it scares me. I give the baby to Enni and make her promise to watch our child as I follow behind the men and my children. We stop upon a hill below the valley at a cave entrance. My blood runs cold. I once again sense the shadow of an insatiable hunger, but it no longer lies hidden in the darkness of the cave. It stands in the sunlight. It covers Erikka's children with its embrace.

Chapter
12
Destiny

The snow from winter continues to give way to spring. The cave looks dark even with the sunlight high above us. I watch my green-eyed friend perched on the warrior's shoulder. With a laugh, he looks up and flies over, landing beside me as he does. It is here we watch the next part of the plan unravel.

The men toss torches into the cave, and I see the first stirrings of the monsters within. The first to come out is the monster that was once my mother. She snarls and swipes with her blood and dirt covered hands, throwing a skull that has been picked clean. One of the men throw a spear, but it misses, landing just shy of her grotesque frame.

More monsters come out of the cave to join my mother. I don't remember there having been so many before. It's not long before the fight begins. Eemil and my children lead, some turning into their bear form. Others fight as men, but with far more strength and power than the humans we share the field with—who we were *forced* to fight with. I say forced, but I can sense that something has changed.

My children and mate are naturals on this battlefield. There is a beauty in the fierceness in which they fight and hand out death. It appears as if there is some joy in it, and my heart sinks at that revelation. I know well the feeling of the bear power coursing through me. I think back to those first few days in the woods by myself soon after the change, and how much joy it brought me to flex my power. The joy in knowing I could hunt, that I could kill whatever I wanted to. That I had the strength to topple trees.

"They're beautiful, aren't they?" a man's voice says from beside me.

I look over at a man with black hair, pale skin, and bright green eyes and I know it is my green-eyed friend. There is not a doubt in my soul of such a thing.

"They're made to fight. You should be proud." I follow where his finger points, and it lingers on Eemil. "Look at them," he says, and I do. I also see the human warriors standing back and watching too.

"Take a look, Spring Maid. This is the moment where you lose everything. He is a sight to behold out there on the battlefield—a creature made for glory. Ole one-eye will ride down himself when that one falls. But he made you too good. You made them too good. The would-be king has taken notice, and now he will take all of you. Slaves. Your line will end."

He laughs, the sound so familiar, but instead of comforting me as it did so many months ago, it sends a chill down my spine.

"Why are you against me?" I Ask.

He does not reply, but merely smiles—a wicked smile.

"My name is Berja," I say quietly, no longer sure of the power in a name.

"Are you sure, mother of monsters?"

"We're not monsters."

"Are you sure? It's hard to tell the monster apart from the man on the battlefield."

"Why are you against me?" I ask again.

"I'm not usually one for the long game, but a war is coming between the gods and the giants." He shrugs, that smile still on his lips. "I stand with my children. I need to ensure Odin's plan with you will fail. Sure, he may have gained a few great warriors, such as your mate out there, but no great army will come from you. He is destined to lose. I intend to keep destiny's path clear. Surely you can understand that as a mother, even one of monsters."

Suddenly, an intense pain shoots through my abdomen. A large, sharp needle from a mistletoe sticks from my stomach and a dark red color expands around it. Terror turns my limbs cold at the fatal sight.

"Mistletoe has always been my favorite," he acknowledges. "It's amazing how plants can grow with some kind words and encouragement. Such an easy, unassuming weapon. Even a blind man can be lethal with it."

I pull out the needle as he caresses my face with his long white fingers.

"Don't worry, dear one," he whispers. "It'll be over soon. This will have been but a dream."

I turn to run but collapse instead. The man behind me laughs, even as a bird takes his place. My green-eyed friend, who I once trusted, flies to sit again upon the warrior's shoulder. A single caw from his feathered throat echoes across the field, and in my deteriorating state, I can't help but think it was the sound of celebration.

The battle is soon over, and the threat from Erikka's rage becomes a horrid memory. Nothing of her is left now. I see the smiles and hear the whoops and yells from my children down below. I watch the warriors surround them and the leader get down from his horse to praise them. I can almost see the poison of the words he spins rope them in, and I know what the green-eyed bird said will be true: there is a hunger in them that has been unleashed.

I am just a Spring Maid after all, and I have done my duty.

There is little I can do for them. I can only run, and so I force myself up and stumble back to the village. I keep going until I am racing down the path to the altar, my breaths ragged and the blood everywhere.

"Help me!" I cry. My strength is waning. I'm growing weaker by each fading heartbeat. Agony turns to numbness.

I thought I only wanted my freedom to save them. I failed at both. They took my words and changed the meaning, then blamed me for creating the monsters they turned into.

"I had warned you of what could happen." It is Dream Mother who finally arrives, her voice grave.

"Yes, but I thought I could save them all, but I have doomed them—those I loved, my children, everyone who counted on me. I wanted to do good. I wanted to save the Spring Children."

"You cannot save those who are unwilling, who refuse. To try is folly. You will get another chance though. Two will come for you, and you will have to decide who to save. For now, dear Berja, sleep. Sleep and forget, mother of bears."

"Mother of bears? No, mother of monsters. That is what they will call me for that is what I am." I say as my breathing shifts into sporadic bursts.

Snowflakes start to fall around me—a late spring snow that should not be. I feel my body begin to pull into the ground where I lay before the altar. There is a force beckoning me, dragging me under without my consent.

My skin and bones turn painfully into roots that shoot into the earth. The tendrils of my body find and wrap around the bones of my brothers and sisters buried below me. My spine snaps and shoots up toward the sky, and my skin hardens into the bark of an ash tree.

The Dream Mother continues to speak as the snowflakes fall atop my trunk and leafy crown, "The snow is a blanket. Lay under its cover and give yourself to its coldness. Your time will come again."

About the Author

J.K. Divia is a mom and wife from Baltimore, Maryland. with a degree in Communications and minor in Anthropology. J.K has spent time traveling both in the United States and Europe. She is a Spoonie and has learned the importance of rest while pursuing her writing dreams. As a child she was obsessed with world mythology, folklore and ghost stories which have influenced her writing. She has always loved creative writing and once she decided to take it beyond flash fiction writing contests, she found a writing coach and editor to help her achieve her goal of writing and publishing her stories. A Sea of Blood and Tears was her debut novel.